#8 TWO FRIENDS TOO MANY

D0556388

**Look for these and other books
in the PEANUT BUTTER
AND JELLY series:**

#8 TWO FRIENDS TOO MANY

Dorothy Haas

Illustrated by Paul Casale

A
LITTLE APPLE
PAPERBACK

SCHOLASTIC INC.
New York Toronto London Auckland Sydney

ISBN 0-590-43557-4

Copyright © 1990 by Dorothy F. Haas. All rights reserved. Published by Scholastic Inc. APPLE PAPERBACKS is a registered trademark of Scholastic Inc. PEANUT BUTTER AND JELLY is a trademark of Scholastic Inc.

12 11 10 9 8 7 6 5 4 3   0 1 2 3 4 5/9

Printed in the U.S.A.   28

First Scholastic printing, October 1990

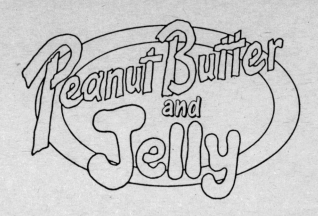

#8 TWO FRIENDS TOO MANY

CHAPTER 1

"Look, Peanut. This letter is for you," said Emmy, hanging her jacket on the post at the foot of the stairs in the Buttermans' front hall. She was looking down at the low chest of drawers that stood there.

"Do you always let letters lie around without reading them?" asked Erin.

"She gets so many letters she forgets to read them," Jilly said, laughing.

"Really? A letter for me?" Peanut's voice was muffled. She was struggling to get out of her jacket. "It must have come today," she said, popping out of the jacket at last, leaving its sleeves turned inside out. She dropped it on the floor. Her little dog Nibbsie curled up on it, let out a contented yip, and closed his eyes.

She dived for the envelope. "Regan!" she shrieked. "It's a letter from Regan!"

Regan lived in Minneapolis. That's where Peanut — called Polly by most grown-ups — had lived before the Butterman family moved to Evanston. Regan and Peanut wrote to each other — but not quite as often as they had at first. They had even talked with each other on the telephone a couple of times. But the phone calls had just been special treats.

Peanut started to tear open the letter. Then she stopped, feeling it. "How funny. The envelope is all lumpy."

Jilly, who was Peanut's best friend, and Emmy and Erin crowded around her, filled with curiosity.

Peanut found a letter opener in the top drawer of the chest and slit open the envelope.

She peeked inside and giggled. "That Regan! Everything's a joke to her!"

She held the envelope over the chest. Bits and snips of paper fluttered onto the shiny wood surface. "It's a letter, all right," said Peanut, still laughing. "Only she cut it up and turned it into a puzzle."

"There must be a million pieces there," said Jilly in awe.

Erin's eyes were wide. "You've got to put it together before you can read it. Hey, that's mean!"

"It is not!" Peanut said firmly. "It's funny. Regan always does funny things. You never know what to expect. She's a barrel of fun."

"Aren't you dying to know what she said?" asked Emmy.

Peanut scooped the bits of paper back into the envelope. "Come on," she said, heading for the kitchen. "My mom made lemon crunch cookies last night. Help me with the letter, and you get a cookie. Don't help, and you can watch me eat them all."

She set the cookie jar on the table and

emptied out the envelope. Nobody paid any attention to the cookies. Everybody hung over the table, sorting out the bits of paper.

"Do you think maybe the white pieces are the back of the letter, like a jigsaw puzzle?" asked Jilly.

"Put the white pieces in one place," said Peanut. "Maybe they're the places between words."

"Look for the pieces with straight edges, like in a puzzle," said Emmy.

"Here," said Erin. "Doesn't this look like a *t*?"

"And here's the top of a capital *c* and part of an *h* — I think," said Jilly. "What a mess! I've never seen so many teeny tiny bits. Are you *sure* she doesn't hate you, Peanut?"

Peanut laughed. "Know what I did for her birthday? I sent her a birthday card. And I sent a letter in it. Only I wrote the letter backwards. Is *that* ever hard to do. I had to use a mirror. I knew it would make her die laughing."

"Don't breathe," said Emmy. "That moves

4

the pieces. Look. I think I've got *Dear* here. All I need is part of an *r* that fits."

"This looks like the top of a capital *g* and an *r*," said Jilly.

They worked for ages.

"Got one!" said Jilly. "Look. This says *trip*."

"Me, too," said Emmy. "I've got most of *present*."

Suddenly Erin began to take quick breaths. Her face screwed up. "Ah-ah-ah — "

"Don't sneeze!" they all yelled. "You'll blow away the letter."

Peanut clapped a paper napkin over Erin's face.

" — choooo!" sneezed Erin.

"What we need is some Scotch tape," said Jilly. "We can tape together the words we finish, and it won't matter if someone sneezes."

Peanut ran to find the tape. When she came back, they put each word on its own piece of tape.

Slowly the mound of bits and pieces grew smaller. With fewer bits to sort out, the words came more quickly. At last there was only a pile of words on the table and some white bits with no writing on them. Regan's letter was finished quickly after that.

Dear Peanut,

I miss you like anything. My grandma knows that. Guess what she gave me for my birthday. A trip to see you! My mom says I can only come if you invite me, though. So hurry up and ask me to come see you. I will fly to Chicago. I have never flown anywhere all by myself. My grandma says I'm old enough to do that now. You and your mom will have to meet me at the airport.

Please write soon and tell me if I can come. If you don't invite me, I will use my grandma's present to fly to Disney World all by myself. Yuk yuk.

Love,
Regan

P.S. You wrote my birthday letter backwards. I'm going to get even, so I'm cutting this letter into pieces. I hope you have fun putting it together. Yuk yuk yuk.

* * *

Peanut's eyes were starry. "Ohhh," she breathed. "How wonderful. I haven't seen Regan since last summer when we moved. You'll all get to meet her. You will just love her. I can hardly wait to ask my mom."

She didn't notice that Jilly was very quiet. What was Jilly to think about Peanut's friend from faraway Minneapolis? Would she "just love" her? Jilly had to think about that.

They had some of the lemon crunch cookies then, and played with Nibbsie until it was time for everyone to go home.

Peanut called Jilly that evening.

"She can come," she said, before Jilly barely had time to say hello. "My mom says it's okay. And guess what else! We're going to have a sleepover on that Saturday night. My mom says she'll have to be home for the whole weekend anyway, so she might as well bite the bullet and have everybody here. There'll be you and Emmy and Erin."

"Neat," said Jilly.

"I can hardly wait for you to meet Regan,"

said Peanut. "Just think. My two very best friends in the whole world are going to meet each other."

"Wow," said Jilly.

"I'm going to write to Regan tonight," said Peanut. "Our moms are going to talk on the phone and decide what weekend is best." She giggled. "My mom said I'd better not write the letter backwards, or she won't know I'm inviting her. Only I know she'll figure it out. She's smart, and she likes jokes as much as I do."

"Oh," said Jilly.

"Gotta go now," said Peanut. "There's just time to write my letter before bedtime."

" 'Bye," said Jilly.

Peanut wrote her letter and went to sleep, smiling into the darkness, thinking about Regan.

Jilly played with her cat, Bumptious, until bedtime. She went to sleep, but she wasn't smiling into the darkness. She was thinking about Regan, too.

CHAPTER 2

The days dragged, but the letters flew.

"I'm coming! I'm coming!" wrote Regan. "I'm going to bring Gumbo. Do you think he and Jumbo will still remember each other?"

Gumbo and Jumbo were twin teddy bears. Peanut and Regan had gotten them the Christmas they were four.

"Sure, Jumbo will remember Gumbo," Peanut wrote back. "I talk to him about Gumbo sometimes. But I can hardly wait for you to meet Nibbsie."

10

Regan knew all about Nibbsie. Peanut had sent her pictures of him. "Tell your puppy that he cannot take a bite out of Gumbo," she wrote. "I looked on the map. You are south of Minneapolis. It must be warmer there. Should I bring my swimsuit? Can we go swimming in Lake Michigan?"

"We can swim in the lake," Peanut wrote, "if we join the Polar Bear Club and wear woolen underwear. It's cold here, Regan, just like in Minneapolis. No, do not bring your swimsuit. Here's what to bring — makeup. Have you got any? Ceci gave me some samples she doesn't want." Ceci was Peanut's oldest sister.

"I've made a present for you," wrote Regan. "It took a long time."

"I'm making a list of things to do," wrote Peanut. "You can choose which ones you want to do. I wish the days would go faster."

"My bag is all packed," wrote Regan. "Only I have to keep opening it to get things I need."

Regan went to sleep nights, thinking about visiting Peanut.

Peanut went to sleep nights, thinking about Regan coming to visit.

Jilly went to sleep nights, wondering, wondering, petting Bumptious. "Will Peanut still like me, Bumpy," she asked one night, "when Regan gets here?"

Bumptious pushed at Jilly's cheek with a paw. "I like you," she seemed to be saying.

Daytimes, the girls talked about what they would do during Regan's visit.

"She's just got to go to the Museum of Science and Industry," said Emmy. "Would she be scared to go down in the coal mine? It's pretty dark."

"If it was summer we could go to Great America and ride the roller coaster," said Erin.

"The glass elevators at Water Tower Place," said Jilly. "I just love them. Maybe she's never ridden in a glass elevator."

Peanut wrote fast, adding the things to her list. "I bet she'd like the old Chicago fire at the Historical Society. You know — you push a button and watch Chicago burn down for a while."

"Don't forget the zoo," said Jilly, looking over Peanut's shoulder. "The koala bear is there now. Maybe she's never seen a koala bear."

The list grew longer and longer. The dinosaurs at the museum. The touching bone. Peanut's school, the Louisa May Alcott. The sky show at the planetarium. The leaning tower of Pisa that wasn't in Pisa, Italy, at all, but right in Illinois on the way to the airport. Peanut worked on her list before and after school.

She was erasing something from it — something she was going to surprise Regan with — one evening. Her mother was sitting beside the fire knitting a sweater for Peanut. Her sister Maggie, who was older than Peanut but younger than Ceci, was doing homework at the desk in front of the windows.

Mrs. Butterman glanced at Peanut's list. "That's getting pretty long, don't you think?"

"It's only four pages," said Peanut.

Maggie shouted with laughter. "Four pages! I thought," she said in an I'm-more-grown-up-

13

than-you voice, "that Regan was just coming for a weekend. You've got enough planned for a month."

Why did Maggie always have to act as though she were more grown-up than Peanut? Sometimes Peanut had to work hard not to let Maggie see what a pain in the neck she was. "She is," said Peanut in a sensible sort of voice. "But a month wouldn't be so bad." She grinned. "Mom, let's ask Regan to come for a whole month next summer."

"I . . . don't . . . know," said Mrs. Butterman, counting stitches between words, "whether . . . I'm . . . up to that. As I think back, the two of you got into enough mischief when you were together to turn a dear old mother's hair gray."

"That was when we were little," Peanut said with great dignity. "We're pretty grown-up now."

Maggie let out a laughing sort of snort, closed her book, and got up to turn on the television. "Says who?"

"You sound funny when you snort," said

Peanut. Maggie really did try her patience. "You're not so much older than me."

"I don't snort," sniffed Maggie. "And I am a whole lot older than you."

"Aren't," said Peanut.

"Am too," said Maggie.

"Girls, don't bicker," said Mrs. Butterman. "Maggie, see if you can find something funny to watch. I'd enjoy a good laugh."

"Don't forget," said Maggie as she flicked through the TV channels, "that you promised I could spend the Regan weekend at Andrea's house." Andrea was Maggie's best friend.

"I won't forget," said Mrs. Butterman. She sighed. "I wonder if Andrea's mother knows what she has let herself in for."

"Mo-ther," moaned Maggie, "don't treat me like a baby."

"Yes, dear," said Mrs. Butterman, smiling and counting stitches.

Nibbsie jumped up beside Peanut on the sofa. "You think I'm pretty grown-up, don't you, Nibbs?" Peanut whispered.

16

Nibbsie kissed the tip of her nose, and Peanut went back to working on the list. She fixed it so that the best things, like the Egyptian mummies, came first.

At the Matthewses', Jilly talked to Bumptious that evening, too.

"Listen, Bumpy," she said as she got ready for bed. "I wonder if I'm going to like Regan." She cuddled Bumptious and rubbed her chin on top of the cat's silky, furry head. "What if I don't like her? What if she doesn't like me?"

"Meow," said Bumpy, who didn't like being held tight. She wriggled out of Jilly's arms and streaked toward the door.

Jilly leaped to close it, but Bumptious got through it first.

"All right for you, Bumpy," Jilly called after her. "See if I care if you don't want to stay here with me."

But she left the door open a crack. Later, when the lights were off, a gray shadow slid silently back into the room, jumped up on Jilly's bed, and stretched out at her feet.

The weeks did pass, and then the days. Five. Four. Three. Two. One.

Mrs. Butterman came to school on Friday to pick up Peanut. Peanut got to leave class early so they could be on their way and not get caught in rush-hour traffic. They didn't want to be late getting to the airport. They meant to be standing right there at the gate, watching people come off the plane, waiting for the first glimpse of Regan.

They did get to O'Hare in plenty of time. Peanut kept looking at the clock in the car and then at all the clocks at the airport. There wasn't time to stop for a Coke, though, which she had kind of hoped would happen.

"Mom," she said as they waited at the arrivals gate, "you know how people always say 'My, how you've changed'?"

"Mm-mm," said Mrs. Butterman, her eyes on passengers starting to come through the gate from the plane.

"What if," said Peanut as people pushed past them, "Regan has changed so much that we don't recognize her?" The thought was so horrible that her stomach scrunched up. She could hardly keep from hopping up and down.

Mrs. Butterman gave her a quick squeeze. "Honey, I don't think there's the least chance in the world that — "

CHAPTER 3

■■■■■■■■■■■■■■■■
　■　■　■　■　■　■　■　■

"Regan!" shrieked Peanut as she caught sight of Regan.

"Peanut!" shrieked Regan.

The two girls rushed past the people in the crowded walkway and flung themselves at each other.

"You haven't changed one single bit, Regan," said Peanut.

"You're exactly the way I remembered you," said Regan. "Oh, I thought I'd never get here!"

They hugged and danced in a circle, laughing.

The crowds of travelers, smiling at so much gladness, parted and flowed around them.

"Somehow," said the flight attendant who had walked from the plane with Regan, "I don't think I have to worry that I'm turning this girl over to the wrong family." She was smiling, too, watching Peanut and Regan.

Mrs. Butterman laughed. "You guessed it! Those two have known each other since they were babies. I do thank you for keeping an eye on Regan. I worried about her traveling by herself."

The pretty young woman handed over Regan's carry-on bag. "It was fun having her. She was so excited about this visit. 'Bye, Regan," she called, raising her voice. "Have fun."

Regan tore herself away from Peanut. "Maybe," she said thoughtfully as she shook hands, "I'll be a flight attendant someday — if I decide not to be a rock star."

She waved at her new friend as she headed back toward the plane. Then she stopped and picked up the box she had dropped when she hugged Peanut. "I hope none of them broke," Regan said mysteriously. She grinned at Peanut. "This is your present."

Peanut hoped so, too — whatever the present was. The box was big and square, so the present had to be big. Unless it was all wrapped up in tissue paper, and then it could be pretty small. But wait a minute — Regan had said "none of them," so the present was more than one of something.

Regan didn't offer the present to Peanut, and so Peanut tried to be polite and not stare at it. That was hard, really hard. "I've got a present for you, too," she said. "Only it's at home."

All the way home, Peanut had to pretend she wasn't sitting there in the car right beside a present. It was a terrible trial! Fortunately there were things for Regan to see, and that took Peanut's mind off the mysterious box.

"Close your eyes," said Peanut as they got near a particular place.

Regan squeezed her eyes shut.

"Soon," said Peanut, "sooon. . . . Mom, you've got to slow down or she'll miss it. Okay, now! Open your eyes."

Regan opened her eyes, not sure what she was supposed to be looking for.

"There!" Peanut pointed. "Look! It's the Leaning Tower of Pisa!"

Regan stared, her eyes round. "It looks like it's going to fall over any minute. Why? What's it for? What happened to it?"

Peanut shrugged. "It was built that way. I guess somebody liked the one over in Italy, so they built one exactly like it."

"Cray-*zeee*!" said Regan. "If the one in Italy falls down before I get to see it, I will at least have seen this one. I mean, it's really kuh-RAY-zee!"

The car picked up speed. Regan looked back until she could no longer see the Leaning Tower.

Peanut dug her list out of her pocket and offered it to Regan. "You can choose anything on this list," she said. "We'll do as many of them as we can tomorrow. Jilly is going to come with us. I'm dying for you to meet Jilly. Then tomorrow night we're going to have a sleepover. Emmy and Erin are going to come."

Regan took the list, reading. She bounced on the seat, even though the seat belt was fastened around her. "Glass elevator," she read. "Is it really made of glass? Oh, look — there's something here about mummies. More than anything in the world" — she clutched the list to her chest — "I'd love to see real mummies."

"There are even cat mummies," said Peanut.

"No!" Regan lifted her eyes from the list. "Real cats? Oh, I've got to see those, too."

"Well, they're not real cats anymore," said Peanut. "They used to be, you know, before they got pickled or whatever they do to turn them into mummies. Thousands and thousands of years ago."

"How do they know the mummies are cats?" asked Regan. "I mean, how do they know they weren't dogs or foxes or something else?"

Peanut wasn't sure. "That's what the sign

at the museum says. Mom," she asked, "how do they know?"

"They unwrapped a few, I think," said Mrs. Butterman, talking over her shoulder, her eyes on the road.

"I don't think I'd like to do that." Peanut wrinkled her nose, thinking what an un-wrapped cat mummy must look like. "Ick!"

"I think they X-rayed them, too," said Mrs. Butterman. They had turned onto a tree-lined street. "The Egyptians took their cats very seriously."

"So do I," said Regan. Then she saw some-thing else on the list of things to do. "Dinosaur bones," she gasped.

"It's a really big one," said Peanut, grinning. "I mean, it's huge."

"Oh, I've got to see the bones," said Regan, awed.

"We're almost home," said Peanut. "Look, down that street, that's where Jilly lives. And around the next corner . . . there . . . there . . . look quick" — she pointed — "my grandpa and grandma live there."

"Why, this looks just like Minneapolis," said Regan. She sounded disappointed. "It doesn't look different here at all."

"Home," said Mrs. Butterman, parking at the curb.

"Come see where I live," said Peanut, running up the walk toward the quaint old house with its high, peaky roof and diamond-paned windows.

Regan followed her, carrying the present. Inside the front door, she held it out. "This is a — " she started to say.

Nibbsie came racing into the hall from the kitchen. He circled their feet, barking fiercely.

Regan held the box high, to keep it safe, looking down at him. He resembled a fluffy stuffed toy. It's hard to take a stuffed toy seriously. "Wow!" she said, "an attack dog. I'm scared to death."

Peanut picked him up. "Nibbsie," she scolded, "don't you bark at Regan. She didn't come to rob us or something."

Nibbsie let out a few more yips, as though to say, "Don't tell me how to protect my house."

27

"Regan," Peanut went on, talking over Nibbsie's head, "I want you to meet His Nibs. Nibbsie" — she held him up and looked into his eyes — "Regan is my oldest best friend. We've known each other since we were two years old."

Nibbsie growled.

Regan stretched out her hand. "I think he smells Rover." Rover — that was Regan's cat. Regan didn't name things like anybody else in the world. A cat is supposed to be called Muffin or Clover or something. But Regan's cat had a dog's name.

Nibbsie sniffed at Regan's hand.

"He'll get used to you," said Peanut. "Now, Nibs, you be nice." She eyed the package Regan still carried.

Regan remembered the present. "This is a house gift — that's what my mom called it. So now that I'm in your house, here it is."

Peanut lowered Nibbsie to the floor and took the box. She felt suddenly shy. Why did getting presents always make a person feel shy? "Golly, Regan, I bet this is something I'll really love."

Regan giggled. "I know you will. You always did. It took me a really long time to get so many."

Peanut tugged off the ribbon and lifted off the cover. She looked into the box and flopped down on the bottom step, bent over, laughing. The box was filled with little packets of crackers, the kind that come with soup at a restaurant. There were dozens and dozens — maybe even hundreds — of the packets.

"You always liked those." Regan was looking pleased. "I started collecting them for you when you moved away. Pretty soon everybody was bringing them to me. There are even lots of the little round kind in there, the ones you liked best of all."

"Regan, you are a nut," gasped Peanut. But she could not help feeling good about the boxful of crackers. Only somebody who knew you really well and thought about you a whole lot would go to the trouble of saving all those little packages just because they knew you loved them. Regan had been thinking about her, for sure!

"I've got something for you, too," she said. "Only it's upstairs in my room. Come on." She started up the stairway.

Mrs. Butterman had come in and was in the living room, kneeling in front of the fireplace. "As soon as I get this burning I'll make us something hot to drink," she called. "Don't stay upstairs too long."

Peanut and Regan raced up the stairway. Peanut led the way into her room. Regan skidded to a stop in the doorway. "You've got a windowseat," she squealed. She went to it and knelt on the flower-covered cushion, looking outside. "Awesome," she breathed. "Totally awesome."

"That tree out there," said Peanut, "belongs to me, just me. It's my tree. When there are leaves on it, you feel like you're sitting right in the tree. There's a nest, too. It's left over from last summer. Maybe it's for robins. You've got to come back in summertime so you can see the robins."

Regan was polite, as polite as Peanut had been. Peanut had said there was a present up here. Where was it? Was there something that had *present* written all over it? She looked around, remembering the bunk beds, the chest of drawers, Peanut's old teddy bear Jumbo sitting on top of the chest. "It is and it isn't like Minneapolis in this room," she said. But she tried to look as though she wasn't looking for a present.

"Mm-mm," said Peanut, digging around in the top drawer of the chest. "I wish I could hurry up and be twelve. Then I'm going to get new furniture, and I'll get to pick it out." She pulled a floppy tissue-paper package out of the drawer. "For you," she said, offering it to Regan.

Regan didn't believe in untying bows and folding gift paper. She ripped open the package and held up a T-shirt. On the front was a picture of a curly-haired toddler sticking out her tongue. THE TERRIBLE TWO said the words under the picture.

Regan giggled. "We sure were terrible." She pulled off her sweater. "That's what our moms called us."

"Remember the time we took all the grass clippings and put them in your mom's clothes dryer?" asked Peanut.

Regan was halfway into the T-shirt. "And the time we painted mud pictures" — her head popped out — "all over the side of your dad's car?"

Peanut pulled on an identical T-shirt. "I got one, too," she said, "and there's one for Jilly. Only you can't see it until tomorrow."

"But she's not two," said Regan, puzzled. "She makes three."

"You'll see," said Peanut. And that's all she would say.

"Girls?" The call came from downstairs. "Come now before this cools off."

Peanut and Regan went downstairs in their matching T-shirts. Mugs of hot apple cider were on a tray in front of the fireplace.

"Remember Mrs. Torkelsen at Halverson School?" asked Regan. "She's not there any-more."

"Why not?" asked Peanut. Mrs. Torkelsen had been at Halverson School forever. She had taught Ceci and Maggie, before she taught Peanut.

"She had a baby," said Regan. "She brought him to school so we could see him. He's got the bluest eyes, and his name is Leif. She stays home now and takes care of Leif."

Peanut stirred her cider with a cinnamon stick. "Remember how we met?"

Regan's forehead puckered. "I don't think I really remember. I think I just heard about it and think I remember."

"Mom?" asked Peanut, who never tired of hearing the story. "Tell us about how we met."

Mrs. Butterman had gone to the piano and started to play. "Mmm?" she asked, a dreamy look on her face.

"Tell about how we got to be friends," said Peanut. "You know."

Mrs. Butterman paused, her hands over the keys. "Regan's mother and I happened to be in the cereal aisle at the supermarket one day."

"But you didn't know each other," Peanut prompted her.

"We didn't know each other," Mrs. Butterman agreed. "We were picking out cereal. The two of you started pulling boxes off the shelves, scattering them on the floor, running down the aisle, laughing like little fiends. When we finally caught up with you, the two of you held hands and would not let go."

"And we were friends forever after," said Regan.

"You were two years old," said Mrs. Butterman. "That's a difficult age — the terrible twos."

She went back to playing the piano, and Peanut and Regan went back to remembering all of the things they had shared since they were two years old.

CHAPTER
4

■▪■▪■▪■▪■▪■▪■▪■▪■▪■▪■▪■

Peanut woke up in a daze. Where was she? Why was she way up here near the ceiling? What . . . what . . ? A plushy bundle bounced off the ceiling and landed beside her.

"Hey, Jumbo," said a deep voice. "It's me, Gumbo. Remember me?"

Regan's head appeared at the end of the upper bunk. She was standing on the ladder.

Peanut was instantly wide awake. Regan was here, in her very own bedroom. Regan!

"Sure, Gumbo," she replied in her own deepest voice. "Us bears never forget our twins."

35

She set Gumbo and Jumbo beside each other on her pillow.

Regan crawled up onto the bed and sat cross-legged. "I thought you'd never wake up. How come you sleep so much? You never used to sleep long in the morning."

Now, how could a person answer that! Peanut yawned and stretched. "I guess I'm not used to talking so late at night."

They had talked until Mrs. Butterman came into the room in her robe, looking sleepy, and said, "Enough now, or you'll be too tired to enjoy yourselves tomorrow." She had flipped off the light.

What had they decided last night? "So what you want to do today," said Peanut, sorting things out in her mind, "is see where I go to school — "

"Uh-huh," said Regan.

" — and see the lake," Peanut went on.

"Right," said Regan.

"And then go see the mummies — "

"Especially the cat mummies," Regan broke in.

" — and the dinosaur bones — "

"Mummies and dinosaur bones all in one place! Maybe Chicago is a pretty good place after all." Regan thought for a moment. "You live in Evanston. Are Chicago and Evanston the same place?"

"Practically," said Peanut. "The edge of Chicago and the edge of Evanston bump into each other." She continued with the day's plans. "Then we'll ride the double-decker bus."

"Inside or outside?"

"Outside," said Peanut, "up on top. Even if it's freezing or snowing or — "

The telephone rang downstairs.

" — something," Peanut went on. "It's best up on — "

"Polly?" Mrs. Butterman called from downstairs. "Jilly is on the phone."

"Coming," called Peanut, sliding out of the upper bunk without even using the ladder. She landed on the floor with a thud. "Tell her I'm coming.

"I can hardly wait for you and Jilly to meet each other," she told Regan as she darted from

37

the room. "Come downstairs with me. Say hi on the phone."

She thumped down the stairs barefoot and leaped the last three steps. Regan followed and hung over the railing as Peanut picked up the telephone.

"Jilly!" Peanut said without even saying hello, "we only have to eat breakfast, and then we'll come to pick you up. Mom's going to drive. Regan wants to see the — What? What did you say?"

She listened. The smile faded from her face.

"But that's terrible! Are you sure? Did you look in the — ?"

She listened some more. "We'll come help you look," she said. "Right away."

She put down the phone and stood without moving, rubbing one bare foot against the other to warm it.

"What's up?" whispered Regan. Something had to be wrong. Peanut hadn't asked her to say hi to Jilly.

"Jilly's cat," said Peanut. "Bumpy got out of the house. Jilly can't find her."

"Ohhhhh," breathed Regan.

"She's looked everywhere," said Peanut. "She's scared, really scared something awful has happened to Bumpy."

Mrs. Butterman looked into the hall from the kitchen. "Breakfast is just about — " She stopped when she saw Peanut's face. "Whatever in the world — ?"

Peanut explained. "We've got to go help Jilly, Mom," she said. "Right away. Before we go to the museum."

"Run upstairs and get dressed," said Mrs. Butterman. "But I won't permit you to leave the house until you've eaten breakfast. Not when you are going to be outdoors in the cold. Hurry. Breakfast will be on the table as soon as you're dressed."

Peanut and Regan raced up the stairs. Forgotten were the wonderful sightseeing plans for the day.

"I don't know who I feel sorrier for," said Peanut, pulling on her jeans, "Jilly or Bumpy. Jilly because she loves Bumpy and is scared, or Bumpy because maybe something has happened to her."

"She loves Bumpy like I love Rover," said Regan, tying her shoelaces. "I'd feel horrible if something happened to Rover."

"But maybe I'm sorriest for Bumpy," said Peanut. "Bumpy — her name is really Bumptious, but Jilly calls her Bumpy or Bumps — she isn't used to being outside. She's a house cat. I don't think she knows how to take care of herself outdoors."

Regan dug around in her suitcase. "I made something for Jilly. Only I don't know if I should give it to her now." She stood for a moment, undecided, biting her lip. "Maybe I can't," she said at last, "but I'll take it with me anyway." She stuffed something — a rattly something — into her jacket pocket and followed Peanut downstairs, rattling at every step.

Mrs. Butterman was at the stove, sliding hotcakes onto plates, when they went into the kitchen. "Peanut," she said, "please pour milk for yourselves. Regan, you will find knives and forks in the drawer beside the sink. Will you put them at your places? And then both of you, sit down."

The girls followed orders and slid into their seats at the table.

Mrs. Butterman put their plates in front of them and set out butter and maple syrup.

Peanut looked at the hotcakes on her plate. They were golden brown. She knew they were going to be delicious. But somehow she just didn't care about them. She could only think about Jilly.

CHAPTER 5

■▼■▼■▼■▼■▼■▼■▼■▼■▼■▼■

"What happened? How did Bumpy get out? Where have you looked? Are you sure she isn't hiding somewhere in the house?"

They were at Jilly's house. They had scarcely got inside the front door before Peanut began peppering Jilly with questions.

"We don't know how she could have got out." Jilly looked worried and unhappy. "Maybe something awful has happened to her. Maybe she's someplace where she needs help. No, she isn't in the house. She — " Suddenly she saw the stranger standing behind Peanut. So this was Regan, wonderful barrel-of-fun Regan. "Uh, hi," said Jilly.

Peanut remembered Regan then. "Regan came to help hunt," she said. "She's got a cat, too."

Another cat person? "You never told me that about her," said Jilly. Her estimate of Peanut's other best friend began to rise. It went up at least five points. Could another cat person be all bad?

"His name is Rover," said Regan.

"Rover!" Jilly's lips quirked upwards at the corners. What a funny name! She added another five points. "Does it make him mad to be called a dog's name? If I were him, my feelings would be hurt. I'd be really, really insulted."

"He never said he didn't like it," said Regan, grinning. "I got him after Peanut moved away. My dad told me I needed somebody to take her place."

"Hey!" protested Peanut. "It takes more than a cat to make up for me. I mean, at least it takes two!" Then she got down to business. "When did you miss Bumpy?"

"She was on my bed for a while last night," said Jilly. "But she wasn't anywhere in the house this morning."

She filled them in on all the places they had looked. "My dad even went up in the attic," she finished. "He thought she might have found a way to get up there between the walls or something. Only she didn't. I mean, she wasn't there."

"Did you look in your clothes dryer?" asked Regan. "Rover jumps into our dryer whenever the door is left open."

Jilly hadn't thought of that. They raced to the basement and the laundry room.

"Bumpy?" Jilly called, turning on the light.

The door of the clothes dryer was shut. Jilly opened it. Bumpy was not inside. Nor was she in the washing machine — Peanut looked. And she wasn't stuck up inside the clothes chute, either — Regan checked that out.

As long as they were looking inside things,

they headed back upstairs to look into the dishwasher and the oven.

"Regan," said Peanut as they bounded up the steps, "you rattle. Did you know you rattle?"

"Rocks," said Regan. "In my head. It happens when I think real hard."

Peanut laughed. That Regan!

The dishwasher was empty — except for some dishes. So was the oven — there wasn't anything in there, not even something baking.

Jerry, Jilly's older brother, came in from outdoors. He pulled off his mittens and slapped them down on the table. "I rode my bike all over the neighborhood. Bumps isn't anywhere around here that I could see."

A yellow cat came silently into the kitchen and wrapped itself around Jerry's ankles.

"Hey!" Regan pointed. "There's your cat."

Jilly shook her head. "That's not Bumpy. That's Jerry's cat, Dr. Blankenstein. My little brother's cat Bonkers is around here someplace, too. Bonkers is a calico. Bumpy is gray."

Jilly's father came into the kitchen. "How's

it going, scout?" he asked. "Any luck?" He studied Jilly's face. "I see. No luck yet."

"We're going outside to look some more," said Jilly. "Dad, can I have a can of tuna fish?"

"That's mighty expensive cat food," said Mr. Matthews. "But I guess we won't worry about that, not today."

He opened the can himself and scraped the tuna into an empty cottage cheese container.

"The top on that needs holes so the fish smell can get out," said Jerry. He was taking his role as big brother of the family very seriously today.

He cut holes in the container top, and Jilly and Peanut and Regan went outdoors. Jilly carried the tuna fish. Bumpy was going to smell it and come.

Jilly shivered. "Bumpy's not used to being outside." Her voice quivered. "And I bet she's hungry by now, too."

They hunted all around the yard, behind every bush, under the porch, in the basement window wells, calling, calling. But a gray shadow moving on silent feet did not come gliding out of any of those places.

"She just has to be somewhere in the neighborhood," said Peanut. "I mean, how far can a cat get to in a couple of hours?"

They combed the neighbors' yards and found a lot of things — a rusty rake lying under some bushes, a Frisbee, a sorry-looking doll that must have spent the winter outdoors. But that's all they did find.

The search took them at last to the park along the lake. They didn't find Bumpy there, either.

Regan looked out over the lake, beyond the huge rocks that lined the shore. "I've never seen such a big lake," she said. "You can't even see the other side. It's practically like the ocean."

Peanut remembered then that the lake was one of the things Regan had wanted to see. She had come yesterday, and she had to go home tomorrow, and maybe all she was going to see on the list of important things was this little part of the lake.

Regan didn't complain, though.

They headed back to the Matthewses' house, looking, looking.

Jilly jogged beside Regan. "You sound kind of like a tambourine, Regan."

"Cha, cha, cha," said Regan, grinning. "My folks do that dance."

Jilly only half listened. She really did not feel like making jokes.

In the backyard, she set the tuna fish on the sidewalk where the wind could blow on it and maybe carry the wonderful smell to Bumpy wherever she happened to be. Inside the house, Dr. Blankenstein and Bonkers, all cozy and warm, sat on the kitchen windowsill and looked out into the cold, gray day.

The girls huddled on the steps glumly, their arms around their knees.

"In storybooks," said Peanut, "when a cat is lost, someone always finds it, and it's had kittens."

Jilly sighed. "Have you ever noticed that real life is hardly ever like storybooks? If this were a story, we'd have found Bumps by now."

A car passed in the alley at the back of the

yard, kicking up pebbles against the garage.

"Cats always get into things," said Regan. "Are there any garbage cans out there in the alley? Did you look in them?"

"Looked," said Jilly without moving.

Another car moved slowly through the alley. It stopped in front of a garage across the way. The garage door slid upward.

Regan sat up straight, her eyes on the car.

The car went into the garage, and the door slid back down.

Regan stood up, her eyes on the garage, and went toward the fence.

"Regan, where are you going?" called Peanut.

Regan didn't answer. Peanut and Jilly ran after her.

Regan fumbled with the latch on the gate, opened it, and went out into the alley. She put her ear against the Matthewses' garage door, listening. She looked like a detective in a mystery story.

After a moment she moved on to the next garage, the one next door.

Peanut and Jilly followed her.

Again Regan bent down, listening at the door. Then she turned to Jilly, smiling. "There's a cat in this garage," she said. "How much do you want to bet it's Bumpy?"

CHAPTER
6

■▀■▀■▀■▀■▀■▀■▀■▀■▀■▀■▀■▀■

Jilly darted to Regan's side. "Bumpy?" she called. "Are you in there, Bumps?"

"Meow." The sound definitely came from inside the garage. More meows followed, here and there, close to the door, as though the cat inside was trying to find its way out.

Jilly's face brightened. "That's Bumpy, all right! I'd know her voice anywhere. But how did she get in there?"

"I bet Mr. Oliver took his car out this morning," said Peanut. "She must have gone inside when the door was open. And she stayed in there when it closed."

"Can you ask the Olivers to open the garage door from inside the house?" asked Regan.

Jilly ran to the back door. She leaned on the doorbell and waited. She could hear the bell ringing faintly, inside the house. But nobody came to the door.

"I don't think anybody's home," she called. She pressed the bell one more time and gave up. "Now what'll we do?" she asked, coming back to Peanut and Regan.

"Wait, I guess," said Peanut. "They have to come home sometime."

"But you don't have to be scared anymore," said Regan. "At least you know where Bumpy is."

Jilly was feeling better and better. Even if they had to wait all day, Bumpy was safe. She hadn't been hit by a car. She wasn't up in a tree somewhere, afraid of a big dog.

"We're going to have to stay right here," she said. "Otherwise, when the Olivers do come home, they'll open the garage door to put away the car, and Bumpy will run out, and then she'll really be lost."

This was beginning to sound like more problems to Peanut. What about lunch? What about if they needed a drink of water? And poor Regan — she was going to have to go home to Minneapolis without seeing even one single mummy.

Jilly's thoughts were still racing. "We need some signs, just to be sure the Olivers don't open the door. I mean, if we're not here. I'll go get some sign stuff."

She ran into the house. "Dad," she called, "we found her! We found her! Only we can't get to her."

She explained. "I think we're going to have to wait all day," she finished. "We're going to make some signs to put on the door, just in case we have to go away for a minute and the Olivers come home. It's okay to take stuff from the studio, isn't it?"

Mr. Matthews was an artist. His studio was on the top floor of the house.

"I'm glad you tracked her down, scout," he

said. "And yes, go ahead with your signs. But remember — you use the kids' paper and the kids' marking pens. Right?"

"Right," said Jilly, and raced up to the studio.

Almost the only things that her father got upset about were people fooling around with his best brushes and taking his best paper, because they were expensive.

She found the big sheets of kids' paper and marking pens and a roll of tape and hurried back downstairs.

"Hold it," said Mr. Matthews as she skidded through the kitchen. He dropped a hand on her shoulder. "It's almost noon. Mom made soup before she left for her meeting. Make a sign or two, but then I want you all to come indoors for lunch."

"But Dad," wailed Jilly, "what if — ?"

"Jerry will be back from the store soon," said Mr. Matthews. "He can wait near the garage while you eat. I'll send him out as soon as he gets here."

Jilly went back to Peanut and Regan. They taped paper onto the garage door and got busy with the marking pens.

DANGER. DO NOT OPEN THIS DOOR. That's what Jilly wrote.

CAT - AS - TRO - FEE wrote Regan. HELP!

BEWARE, wrote Peanut. WILD CAT INSIDE.

"Bumpy isn't wild," said Jilly.

"You want the Olivers to notice the signs?" said Peanut. "They'll see this one, all right." She underlined BEWARE with wavy red lines.

Jilly was just finishing a picture of a gray cat with green eyes when Jerry came to the fence. "Okay, you guys," he called. "Soup's on. Dad said to go inside. I'll wait while you eat.

"But hurry it up, will you?" he said as they filed past him. "I've got a basketball game this afternoon."

They went indoors and peeled off their jackets. Jilly shivered. "It sure is cold."

"Hey," said Regan, "this isn't cold. You ought

to feel what it's like in Minneapolis when it gets cold. It gets so cold it's noisy."

Peanut's head went up. She stared at Regan, but she didn't say anything.

"Noisy?" asked Jilly.

"Well see," said Regan, "the smoke that comes out of chimneys freezes in the air and falls down on the streets in big chunks. It makes this huge racket."

Peanut giggled.

"The mayor turns on this big blower — it's like a hair dryer — up on top of the city hall and it blows on everything and warms things up. Then the smoke goes up in the air again."

Jilly groaned. "That's a terrible joke."

Mr. Matthews was filling soup bowls. "That's one tall tale," he said.

"I wrote that in a story," said Regan. "My teacher liked it."

The back door banged, and Jilly's little brother Jackie skipped into the kitchen. "I had the best time at Mrs. Potter's this morning." Mrs. Potter was Jackie's sitter during the week. Sometimes they did special things on Saturday mornings, too. "We made cookies. She said I could bring home all the ones I licked."

He held up a plastic bag filled with messy-looking cookies. "Everybody can have one."

Nobody said they wanted one of Jackie's cookies.

"Did Bumpy have fun outside?" asked Jackie.

Jilly's eyes opened wide. "How did you know about that? You were at Mrs. Potter's before we missed Bumpy." She began to have a terrible suspicion. Maybe Jackie had . . . oh, *would* Jackie have . . . ?

Jackie snuffled, and Mr. Matthews handed him a tissue. He scrubbed at his nose with it. "When I opened the back door and sniffed outside to see if I needed two pairs of mittens," he said, "Bumpy sniffed, too. She really wanted to go outside."

Jackie had! Jackie was the one who had let Bumpy out of the house. Jackie — her darling little brother — was responsible for this whole terrible, horrible, awful, scary morning!

"So you let her out," Jilly said menacingly. She loved her little brother, but . . .

"I didn't *let* her," Jackie explained. "I guess she decided it wasn't too cold outside. I guess she decided to go out all by herself."

"Jackie," groaned Jilly, "I think I'm going to . . . going to wring — "

"Enough," said Mr. Matthews. "Nobody is going to wring anything. Jackie and I will have a serious talk later. Now eat, everybody." He turned on the radio.

Pleasant noontime sounds filled the kitchen. The teakettle whistled softly on the stove. Music came from the radio. Crackers made crunching noises as Peanut and Regan crumbled them into their bowls.

"Ouch!" said Jackie. "This soup is too hot." He blew loudly into his bowl to cool it. Jilly leaned over and puffed, too, to help him.

After that, Jackie started eating. He slurped. Jilly looked over his head at Peanut and Regan. "I think my mom's going to teach him

61

about not slurping when he gets to kindergarten."

Mr. Matthews was talking on the kitchen phone. "Yes, I did call earlier. Has Mr. Oliver come in yet?"

Jilly stopped eating and swung around in her chair to listen.

"Good. Tell him I'd like to talk with him if he can spare the time. Tell him it's Charlie Matthews." He waited. "Cliff? Glad I caught you. The kids have an emergency here involving your garage. No, no — not a fire. A *small* emergency."

Peanut and Regan put down their spoons and listened, too.

"One of the cats got out this morning and seems to be holed up in your garage. . . . Mmmm, yeah. . . . Well, if you can spare the time, one little girl in this house will think you're a hero. . . . Yeah. Meet you outside. Okay then, See you." He put the phone back in its cradle.

"Mr. Oliver is coming home?" breathed Jilly. "Ohhh!" She leaped to her feet. "We'd better go right out there. We — "

"Slow down, scout," said Mr. Matthews. "He won't be here for half an hour. Eat your soup."

Soup! It was the best soup that Jilly and Peanut and Regan had ever eaten in their whole lives.

CHAPTER
7

■▼■▼■▼■▼■▼■▼■▼■▼■▼■▼■▼■

Jilly and Regan and Peanut were waiting,
lined up in front of the Olivers' garage, when
a perky red sports car turned into the alley.
The car slowed. Mr. Oliver leaned out the
window. "You weren't eager for me to get
here — I can see that!" He held up the garage
door opener. "Okay, here we go."

"Wait. Oh, please wait another second,"
called Jilly.

She knelt in front of the garage door and
put a spoonful of tuna fish on the cement.

"Bumpy?" she cooed. "Doesn't this smell yummy? Here, Bumps."

"Meow," came the answer from inside the garage.

"She smells it," said Jilly. "I think she's right in front of me on the other side of this door."

Peanut and Regan crouched on either side of her, their hands held out to catch Bumptious if she ran past Jilly.

Jerry stood to one side. "I'll play end," he said, "in case she runs past you guys."

"I'll play fullback," said Mr. Matthews.

"Me, too," called Jackie. "I'm helping, too."

"Here we go then," said Mr. Oliver. The garage door whirred and then rumbled upward.

"Bumps!" exclaimed Jilly, reaching for the little gray cat.

Bumpy slipped through her hands and gobbled up the tuna fish.

Jilly waited for her to get every last delicious

bit and then picked her up. "You sure did have me worried, Bumpy," she said as Bumptious tried to crawl up the front of her jacket. "Come on. Let's go into the house where you belong."

She headed for the Matthewses' gate, with Peanut and Regan trailing after her.

"Scout?" Her father's voice followed her. "Aren't you forgetting something?"

Jilly turned and, walking backwards, called, "Thanks, Mr. Oliver." She waved one of Bumpy's paws at him. "Bumpy says thanks, too."

"Glad I could help," called Mr. Oliver. "But tell her not to make a habit of this."

"She heard you," Jilly called. "She's purring."

"The signs?" added Mr. Matthews. "You'd better take down your decorations."

"I will," promised Jilly, "as soon as we get Bumpy in the house."

They straggled into the house, Jilly cuddling Bumpy, Peanut carrying the rest of the tuna fish, and Regan just rattling.

Indoors, Jilly set Bumpy down beside the

water bowls and watched her drink thirstily. Dr. Blankenstein and Bonkers came running to see what was going on. They circled around Bumpy, curious. Then they backed away and ran into the dining room.

"They're sure acting funny," said Peanut, puzzled. "You'd think they'd be glad to see her."

"I'll bet she smells like the garage," said Jilly. "They'll have to get used to her again."

"That means she won't have to share the tuna fish," said Regan.

"Maybe," said Jilly. She took the tuna fish from Peanut and scraped it into one of the food bowls. She sat back on her heels.

Bumpy began to eat. The other two cats came back, but they stayed at a distance, pacing.

Regan had been struggling to pull something out of her pocket. "I wasn't sure I could give this to you, Jilly," she said. "I couldn't have if you hadn't found Bumpy. Only now you have. I made it for you because Peanut wrote to me about you. It's just like the one I made for Rover."

Puzzled, Jilly waited to see what Regan was going to give her.

With a final tug, Regan pulled a mini-mailing tube from her pocket. She shook it and it rattled. "We got a couple of these in the mail," she explained. "They had advertising in them. They were too neat to just throw away. So I tossed out the advertising. And I put some little stones in them. And I closed them back up. This one" — she shook it — "is for you."

Jilly took the tube, beginning to understand. The tube was decorated with cut-out pictures of cats. "It's a toy for Bumpy!" she exclaimed.

Regan grinned. "After Rover got used to it, he learned to push it around and make it rattle. He thinks he's really big stuff."

Jilly laughed. Only a cat person would know that the best present another cat person could get was a present for their cat! "You're something else, Regan," she said. "Really, you're something else."

She put the toy on the floor and rolled it toward Bumpy. Bumpy ignored it. But Dr. Blankenstein pounced and batted it under the table.

They were on their knees, trying to show Bumpy how to play with the toy, when Mr. Matthews came in from outdoors with Jackie trailing after him. "Playing?" said Mr. Matthews, his eyebrow lifted. "Considering all the things you've got planned for today, you kids are being mighty casual."

"The museum!" said Peanut. "We can still go."

"The mummies," breathed Regan. She had given up hope of seeing the mummies.

"What kind of mummies?" asked Jackie. "I want to go, too."

"Da-ad," said Jilly.

Mr. Matthews picked up Jackie and held him up toward the ceiling.

Jackie shrieked in delight. He loved roughhousing with his father.

Mr. Matthews dropped him over his shoulder. "You," he said, heading toward the front of the house and the stairway to the studio, "and I, are going to have a father-son afternoon. No mummies allowed."

"We are?" Jackie's words grew fainter. "What are we going to do?"

Mr. Matthews's answer was lost in the distance.

Peanut made a hasty phone call to her mother. Then they went outside — being careful that Bumptious did not follow them through the door — and pulled the signs off the Olivers' garage door.

They were waiting on the curb when Mrs. Butterman pulled up in the car.

"Mom," said Peanut as they got in, "can we drive around the school on the way? Regan's got to see where we go to school."

Mrs. Butterman did — twice — as Regan looked and looked.

"We go in that door," said Peanut, pointing.

"Our room is there — it's the one with the cut-out snowflakes on the windows," said Jilly.

And then Mrs. Butterman headed toward downtown Chicago. Regan got to see lots of the lake and, off in the distance, the tallest building in the world, as well as other tall buildings. But — most importantly, they did get to the mummies.

CHAPTER
8

They had to go through a real Egyptian tomb to get downstairs where the mummies were. There were lots of things to look at along the way.

"Look!" Jilly pointed at a clay slab with pictures of birds and plants pressed into it. "It says on the sign that that's writing. They did their writing by drawing with a stick in wet sand."

Regan studied it, popping her gum. "Do you suppose Egyptian kids ever wondered how to spell words?" She was very serious. "Maybe they

73

went to their moms and said, 'Mummy' — "

Jilly and Peanut groaned.

Regan was not to be stopped. " ' — Mummy, how do you spell *bird*? Does it have one leg or two?' "

Peanut and Jilly leaned against each other, laughing.

Even Mrs. Butterman — who wanted them to learn something from this visit to the museum — had to laugh. Then she said, "That kind of writing is called hieroglyphics." She said it again, slowly. "Hi-ro-GLIFF-iks."

The girls were still caught up in their jokes.

"I wonder if Egyptian teachers ever got on kids' cases about their writing the way Miss Kraft does with me," said Peanut. "Like, 'Polly, I cannot read your writing in this book report. Try to make your birds better.' "

"Hieroglyphics?" Mrs. Butterman said again, above their laughter. "Will you try to remember?"

"Hieroglyphics," they murmured as they ran to a low pillar. It had a flat glass top to look into.

Far below, as though it were hidden deep inside a long-ago tomb, was the painted gold mask of an Egyptian king. It gleamed in the bright light.

"Some artist made that thousands and thousands of years ago," said Jilly.

"Would you believe there's that much gold in the whole world?" said Peanut.

"Cray-zee," said Regan. Then, sounding disappointed, she added, "But how do we get to see the mummy? I mean, if it's all covered up like that."

"We won't see that exact mummy," said Peanut, who knew the things in the museum very well. "Maybe because he was a king. But there is a mummy downstairs. Come on."

They made their way past the other exhibits, went down a stairway cut out of stone, and reached the lower floor of the museum. Peanut led them straight to the exhibit she remembered. "There," she said, "what did I tell you?"

They were standing in front of a window. On the other side was a mummy. Some of the worn cloth wrappings were open at the top.

"You can see its head!" gasped Regan, staring and staring, forgetting to chew on her gum. "And its teeth. But it's so small! Were all the Egyptians that small?"

Nobody — not even Mrs. Butterman — knew the answer.

"I wonder if the man would have liked knowing that someday people like us would look at him," said Jilly. She tried to imagine being that long-ago man, but she could not.

"They put things in their tombs that they thought they might want after they were dead," said Peanut. "Like lots of gold and their favorite jewelry."

"And their cats?" said Regan. "Where are the cat mummies?"

Peanut led them through the crowd of people — there were many visitors at the museum that day — to the corner where she knew they would find the cat mummies. "The sign says that they found a place with thousands of cats," she said.

Regan was disappointed. Yes, definitely disappointed. She had thought the cat mummies

would be standing up, their backs humped like Halloween cats. "They don't look like cats at all," she said. "Well, maybe their heads do. But the rest of their bodies look just — well . . . stiff . . . with their legs at their sides. They just look all wrapped up."

But she was pleased to find that there were falcon mummies and vultures and geese and even a crocodile. "If I don't see anything else in Chicago," she sighed, "the mummies were worth my grandma's birthday present."

"Hey!" said Peanut. "You're seeing me. Don't I count?"

Regan considered that. "Ten mummies?" she said after a moment. "You're worth maybe ten mummies."

Mrs. Butterman glanced at her watch. "Some decisions have to be made," she said. "We can spend what's left of our time here. Or we can go over to Michigan Avenue and the double-decker bus. Which shall it be?"

Jilly would really have loved a ride on the double-decker bus. She had never done that.

Peanut thought about the McDonald's she

knew was right here in the museum. If they stayed here, maybe they could have a chocolate shake.

But Peanut and Jilly were polite. Regan was a visitor. They let her choose.

"Dinosaur bones," Regan decided. "I've just got to see them." Imagine! Mummies and dinosaurs all in one afternoon.

Peanut and Jilly put aside their ideas about double-decker buses and chocolate shakes. Dinosaur bones it would be.

They took the elevator up to the second floor because Mrs. Butterman said *her* old bones didn't want to climb the stairs.

Peanut could have found her way to the dinosaur exhibit blindfolded. She and her mother came here often on slow Sunday afternoons. There were several ways of entering the exhibit, and she picked the one where they would come at the dinosaur skeleton headfirst. They stood looking up at him.

"What a little head," said Regan. "I mean, for such a huge creature."

"He's more than seventy feet long," said

Peanut, who knew everything there was to know about this dinosaur.

"Longer than four of your bedrooms," said Mrs. Butterman.

"I wonder what kind of noise he made," said Jilly. She thought for a moment. "Only maybe *he* was a *she*. Anyway — do you suppose he roared like a lion or hissed like a snake?"

"Maybe he just stamped his foot to make a noise," said Regan. "I mean, a really big stamp."

"I don't think anyone knows about dinosaur sounds," said Mrs. Butterman. "And I don't think anybody knows what color they were, either. Myself, I like to think they were pink."

"Mom, you're being silly again," said Peanut.

"Am I?" Mrs. Butterman laughed. "Prove it!"

Peanut and her mother talked about it every time they came to the museum. Sometimes Mrs. Butterman thought the dinosaurs might have been blue. Then she changed her mind and thought maybe they were red, or the color of apricots.

It drove Peanut wild! Nobody could really know for certain what color dinosaurs had been.

They walked around, having a quick look at the other creatures in the exhibit. None of them was as exciting as the "big guy," Apatosaurus, though.

As they went downstairs — Mrs. Butterman said going down wasn't as hard on old bones as going up — she pulled on her gloves. "Button up. It's cold outside."

"There's just one more thing Regan's got to see," said Peanut. It was the surprise she had been saving. "Well, not exactly *see*," she added. "But you know what I mean."

"Hurry it up, then," said Mrs. Butterman. "I'll wait at the exit."

"Shut your eyes, Regan," said Peanut. "Give me your hand."

Regan closed her eyes. "Are we going to see another leaning tower?"

Peanut didn't answer.

"I think I know where we're going," said Jilly. She grinned at Peanut and took Regan's other hand.

Regan walked between them, wondering.

After a moment she felt her hands being placed on something hard and cold.

"Open up," said Peanut.

Regan opened her eyes. What was this stony thing she was touching?

"This is a dinosaur bone," said Peanut.

"It's maybe sixty-five million years old," said Jilly.

"It's a bone," said Peanut, "that turned to stone. It's called a fossil."

Regan ran her hands over the immense fossil bone. It was longer than she was tall, and it was thicker than she and Peanut put together. "Wow!" she said. "Oh, wow! A real dinosaur bone, and I'm touching it."

Peanut and Jilly exchanged smiles. They had done something really great for Regan, surprising her with the bone, put here just so that people could touch it.

As they headed for the exit gate, Regan looked back at the bone. "Kuh-ray-zee!" she said. Then she was thoughtful. "Know something? Maybe I won't be a rock star after all." She popped her gum, thinking. "And not an airplane flight attendant, either. Maybe I'll be someone who goes around digging up dinosaurs and finding mummies."

"Cray-zeee!" Peanut and Jilly said together. Neither of them had ever thought about doing that. "Kuh-ray-zee!"

CHAPTER
9

They dropped off Jilly at her house so she could get her pajamas and sleeping bag.

"I'll come to your house as quick as I can," she said when she got out of the car. "I put my stuff in my backpack last night. But I've got to hug Bumpy for a while so she'll know how glad I am that we found her. Maybe then she won't want to get out of the house next time Jackie opens the door."

She ran indoors, and Mrs. Butterman drove on home.

Peanut and Regan only had time to take Nibbsie for a quick run to the park and get back home and put on their *TERRIBLE TWO* T-shirts before the doorbell rang. They opened the door, standing side by side.

Jilly came into the hall and dropped her backpack and sleeping bag. As she pulled off her jacket, she saw the identical T-shirts. Her eyes went from the picture and words on Peanut's T-shirt to those on Regan's shirt. She laughed, because the picture really was silly. But at the same time a gray cloud of funny feelings settled over her. The T-shirts said that Peanut and Regan were two together. Even if they were terrible, they matched — best friends. What about Peanut and Jilly?

Peanut dropped Jilly's jacket over the railing. "Come on up to my room," she said. "There's something there for you. Quick, before Emmy and Erin get here."

Feeling glum, Jilly climbed the stairs, her backpack slung over her shoulder. Peanut's other best friend, Regan, followed, carrying Jilly's sleeping bag.

Peanut held out a floppy paper package. "This is for you."

Wondering, Jilly tore away the paper. Inside was a T-shirt. She unfolded it and held it up. There on the front was that funny little kid again. Under the picture were the words *I'M TERRIBLE TOO*.

Jilly giggled. How totally wonderful to be called terrible! Only your true friend would know that you absolutely needed to be called terrible on this particular day.

She put on the T-shirt, and the three of them lined up in front of the mirror. The words were backwards, of course, but the three toddlers matched. Peanut and Jilly and Regan stuck out their tongues, too.

"Cray-ZEE!" said Regan, laughing.

Downstairs the doorbell sounded.

"It's them, Emmy and Erin!" said Peanut. "Let's show them!"

They rushed downstairs to open the door before Mrs. Butterman could get to it.

Emmy laughed and stuck out her tongue at them.

Erin didn't quite understand, though. "I don't think you're terrible at all," she said, puzzled, frowning.

"That's okay, Erin," Peanut said kindly. "See, Regan and I went through the terrible twos together — that's what our moms said." She looked down and patted the words. "It's about that, and about the way you can spell two of something and that other kind of *too*. And it's about my two very best friends. And — "

"Polly honey," came a call from the living room, "please shut the door. You're letting all of outside inside — it's cold."

Emmy and Erin crowded into the hall, and Peanut closed the door. And then there were lots of things to be done.

They had to go upstairs and unroll their sleeping bags and decide where each would sleep, and then roll them up again and stuff them into the closet to be out of the way.

They had to get out their pajamas. Only Emmy hadn't brought pajamas. She had a pink nightie with lace around the neck and at the wrists.

They had to line up their toothbrushes in the bathroom — five toothbrushes in five pink glasses.

Regan had to find a rock station on Peanut's radio.

Erin had to set out her makeup. Erin could hardly stand having to wait until she would be old enough to wear lipstick. She had brought three of her mother's lipsticks. "And look what I found in my mom's drawer," she said breathlessly. She held up a small package. "Stick-on fingernails! Two of them are gone, so I guess my mom won't want them anymore. We can try them."

"Is Ceci at home?" asked Emmy. "Can we look in her room?"

Peanut's friends all hoped they would be as smart and pretty and full of fun as Ceci was when they got to be fifteen.

Peanut felt glamorous just having a big sister like Ceci, and she loved showing off Ceci's room. She could only do that when Ceci wasn't around, though.

"Ceci's sleeping over at her girlfriend's house

tonight," she explained. "She said they might stop in before they go to the movies. Let's go look now."

They tiptoed — even though Ceci wasn't home — to the doorway of her room and peeked in. With its white four-poster bed and pale-pink comforter, with its rosy rug and posters of rock stars on the walls, it was the kind of room they all dreamed of having someday.

Erin sighed. "And you can just come in here any old time you want!"

"Uh-huh," said Peanut. "Only I'm not supposed to touch things. Ceci's kind of fussy about what I touch when she isn't around."

None of them could blame Ceci. "I'll never let my little sister into my room when I get to be fifteen," said Emmy. She sounded as though she really meant it.

"Maybe," said a voice behind them, "your little sister will feel about you the way you all seem to feel about Ceci. Ever think about that?" It was Mrs. Butterman. She had come into the hall behind them.

Emmy's mouth opened and stayed that way —

she was that surprised. No, that idea had never occurred to her! Her two-year-old sister was a terrible pest.

Mrs. Butterman smiled at Emmy's surprise. "I wouldn't be the least bit surprised if she got to feeling that way about you, Emmy. Now," she went on, "I'm thinking about the pizza I'll be ordering in a little while. I'll ask for everything on it except the things you detest. So tell me. What do you hate?"

Everybody talked at once.

"I hate those little salty fishy things. What do you call them?"

"Little fish?"

"No, silly. I think they're called anchovies."

"Yes. Anchovies. Ugh!"

"Mushrooms. No mushrooms. Why do people think mushrooms are so great? I always think there's an elf under them, and I'm going to bite him in half."

"You're weird, Peanut Butterman — just as weird as you were when you lived in Minneapolis."

"You never know where you might find an

elf," Peanut said, sounding very wise.

"Enough!" said Mrs. Butterman. "What I'm hearing is that you don't want anchovies and mushrooms." She turned away. "I'll put in the order for six o'clock."

"Makeup?" Erin whispered as Mrs. Butterman left to order the pizza. "If we put it on now we can wear it until bedtime."

She led the rush back to Peanut's bedroom, and she helped everyone with the things they had brought from home. Erin was an expert on makeup.

"More blusher," she said to Jilly, eyeing her cheeks.

"I'll look like a clown!" Jilly protested.

"Smooth it out around the edges," said Erin. She studied Peanut's face. "Why don't you try the purple eyeshadow on one eye and the green on the other? Then you'll be able to tell which one is best for you."

"The thing I liked best about dancing school," said Emmy as she put on Hot Coral lipstick, "was that we got to wear makeup when we gave dance recitals."

They crowded around Peanut's mirror, bobbing back and forth to make room for each other.

Suddenly Jilly looked around. "Where's Regan?"

They had all been so busy seeing only their own faces that they had forgotten about each other. Now they looked around. Regan was not in the room.

"Regan?" Peanut called. "Where are you?"

There was silence.

Then Regan's voice sounded from the hall. "Ta-dahhhh!" She imitated a trumpet. "Here I come, ready or not. Ta-dahhhh," she sang again and leaped through the doorway.

She wasn't wearing eyeshadow or blusher. Maybe she had on lipstick — but nobody would have known because her lips were hidden behind a big, black mustache!

Peanut hooted. "Regan, you are just kuh-RAY-zee!"

The mustache moved. Maybe Regan was smiling behind it. But who could tell? "I've always wanted to wear one of these. I've been saving it since Halloween. My mom wouldn't let me wear it then. She made me be a ballerina because I had my costume from our dance recital and it still fit."

Erin was looking shocked that a girl would want to wear a mustache.

Emmy and Jilly were leaning against each other, gasping with laughter.

Regan ran to the mirror. "Don't I look just great? Isn't this the wildest?"

"The wildest," agreed Jilly, giggling. Regan was like nobody she had ever met. She was — a barrel of fun!

Mrs. Butterman passed in the hallway, carrying an armload of towels. "I've never," she said, glancing into the room, "seen so much goo on the faces of five little — " suddenly she saw Regan. She leaned against the door, laughing. "Good grief," she said. "Oh, good grief!"

Regan crossed the room walking stiffly, wobbling from side to side, the way she had seen Charlie Chaplin walk in a funny old movie. The mustache moved — maybe she was grinning. "Neat, huh?" she said.

"Let me get my camera," said Mrs. Butterman. "This you are going to want to remember forever!" She set down the towels and went for her camera.

The first picture she took was of Regan, of course. Then she did one of all of them together, and one of Peanut and Regan and Jilly so that their T-shirts showed.

They crowded around her as the pictures came out of the camera.

"Look at me!"

"Ohhhh! I closed my eyes."

"I love the way we look with makeup."

"Peanut, your eye shadow is two different colors."

"I couldn't decide," said Peanut. "Anyway, there wasn't time to change it."

As they talked, Mrs. Butterman had been looking closely at Regan. "Regan, honey," she asked, "how did you get the mustache to stick onto your face?"

"Gum," Regan said breezily. "See, I chewed it all afternoon to get it just right."

Mrs. Butterman closed her eyes and groaned.

"Oh, dear! I'm not sure the gum will come off easily."

Jilly spoke into the silence that followed. "I blew a great big bubble once. It got almost as big as my whole face. Then it popped and stuck all over my face. My mom got most of it off, but I had little bits of gum for a long time."

"I think I'd like to get to work on that mustache before the pizza comes," said Mrs. Butterman.

"Does it have to come off?" said Regan. She looked sorrowful. "Can't I maybe wear it until bedtime?"

"And eat pizza?" said Mrs. Butterman. "And ice cream?"

"I see what you mean," said Regan. "Ugh!"

They all trooped after Mrs. Butterman and Regan into the bathroom and sat on the edge of the bathtub to watch. Except that Jilly got up and held Regan's hand when the mustache came off.

Regan's eyes watered, but she didn't even say, "Ouch!"

Jilly went on holding her hand as Mrs.

Butterman scrubbed at her upper lip with cold cream.

My two best friends, thought Peanut, watching Jilly and Regan. And they like each other! Is that because they are both cat people? No, she decided. It's because they are *great* people — even though they are so different from each other.

Regan — barrel-of-fun Regan — who always thought of crazy things to do.

Jilly — Jilly who always seemed to know exactly how you felt and shared your feelings with you.

Had any girl ever been so lucky? Two such wonderful friends!

Downstairs, the doorbell rang, and Nibbsie began barking frantically.

"That must be the pizza delivery man," said Mrs. Butterman, still working away on Regan's face. "Polly honey, will you take it? Put it in the kitchen. The money is beside the telephone."

Peanut raced out of the room.

There was this whole wonderful evening to

look forward to before tomorrow and Regan's plane to Minneapolis.

Regan, her oldest friend, in faraway Minneapolis, always there for her no matter how long the time between their visits.

And Jilly, right here, forever and ever.